INTRODUCTION

On Oak Tree Farm, ducks are quacking, hens are clucking, horses are neighing, sheep are bleating, the dog is barking, the cat is meowing ... in fact, *everyone* is making noise. But what exactly are they saying? These *Farmyard Tales* let you in on the secret, and, believe me, there are some strange goings-on among the birds and animals on Farmer Shrive's land. You'll meet lazy ducks and busy hens, daring dogs and shabby sheep, and more mice and bunnies than you might expect in a well-run barnyard.

On Farmer Shrive's farm, you need to keep your ears and eyes open. As you read the stories, can you spot Henrietta Hen's eggs on every page and solve the mystery of what exactly happens to them by the end of the book?

Oh, Farmer Shrive, he had a farm,
E-I-E-I-O!
He kept his animals from harm,
E-I-E-I-O!
With a cluck, cluck here, and a quack, quack there, and a
moo, moo here, and a baa, baa there... Poor Farmer Shrive!

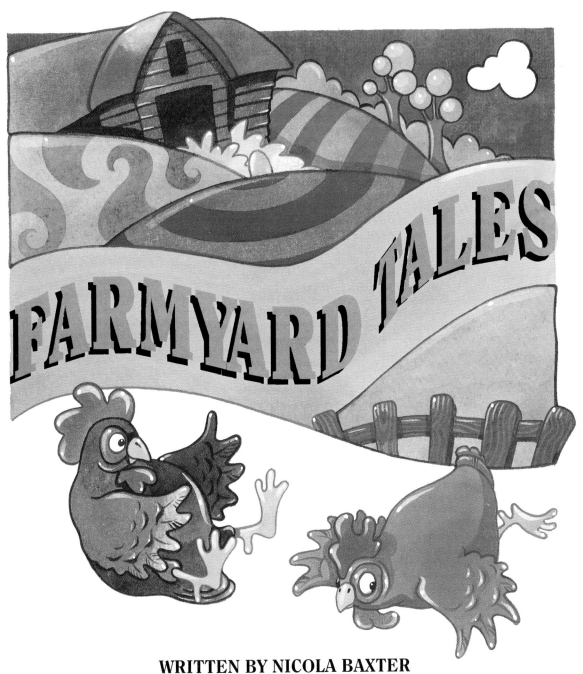

FARMYARD TALES

WRITTEN BY NICOLA BAXTER

ILLUSTRATED BY CATHIE SHUTTLEWORTH

ARMADILLO

FOR DORA SHRIVE
C.A.S.

Published by Armadillo Books
an imprint of
Bookmart Limited
Registered Number 2372865
Trading as Bookmart Limited
Desford Road
Enderby
Leicester
LE19 4AD

ISBN 1-84322-014-8

Produced for Bookmart Limited by Nicola Baxter
PO Box 215
Framingham Earl
Norwich, Norfolk
NR14 7UR

Designer: Amanda Hawkes
Production designer: Amy Barton
Editorial consultant: Ronne Randall

Printed in Singapore

CONTENTS

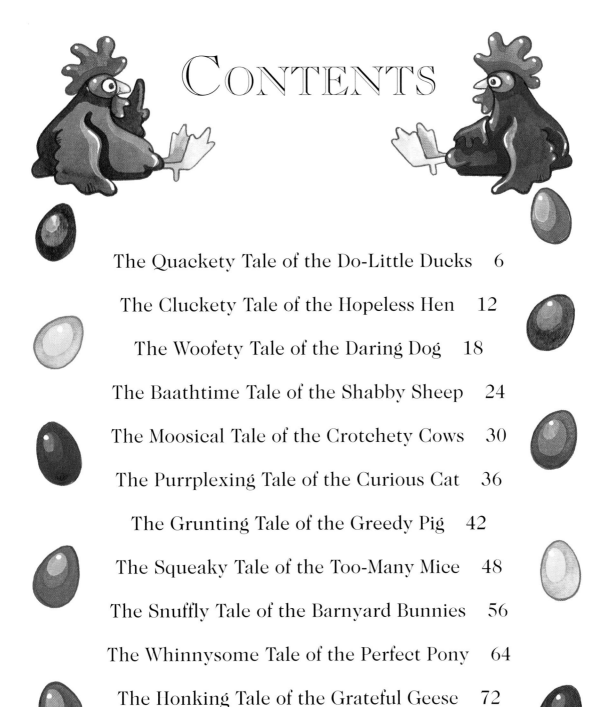

The Quackety Tale of

THE DO-LITTLE DUCKS

Henrietta Hen scratched in the dust. You could tell she was annoyed.

"They're at it again!" she clucked, glaring at the ducks with her beady little eyes. "Look at them!"

"At what?" asked Rudgeworth the rooster. "They're not doing anything, as far as I can see, my dear."

"*Eggsactly!*" The irritated hen looked triumphant. "They never do do anything. The rest of us are working our wings off, night and day. I've laid an egg each morning since they were ducklings. Mrs. Moo has given enough milk to fill the pond. And what do those do-little ducks do? Less than a little! Nothing at all! It shouldn't be allowed on a busy farm."

Down by the pond, half a dozen ducks were dozing on the bank, while some fluffy ducklings tried out their swimming skills under the watchful eye of Durwood, the oldest drake on the pond. Suddenly, with a lot of squawking and flapping, all the ducks woke up and dashed into the water for a splash.

Henrietta Hen put her beak in the air and clucked disapprovingly. "Idlers and hooligans," she sniffed.

Henrietta herself was always very busy. At that particular moment, she was trying to find a safe place to lay her eggs. If she put them in the henhouse, Farmer Shrive would want them for his breakfast. Henrietta wanted to find a nice, quiet spot where she could sit safely on her eggs until they hatched. For a hen with important matters like that on her mind, distracting, diving, dabbling, ducking, daydreaming ducks were very annoying.

Luckily, that afternoon, Henrietta found just what she was looking for. On the opposite bank of the pond, under an old apple tree, someone had left a basket. It was almost hidden in the long grass. Henrietta hopped inside to try it out. It would make a perfect, hen-shaped hatchery.

With Henrietta otherwise occupied, things were a little quieter in the farmyard—but not much. Those do-little ducks were still making a lot of noise. Henrietta glared at them through the holes in her basket.

"Useless!" she muttered. "What good is being able to swim? *I've* never needed to do it."

A week later, nothing much had changed except the weather. Big dark clouds had gathered in the sky and a brisk breeze was ruffling the water of the duckpond. Henrietta huddled in her basket to protect the growing number of precious eggs under her warm, smooth feathers.

That night, the wind blew stronger. It whipped
the grass flat under the apple tree. Worse still,
Henrietta found her basket beginning to rock. It
was not nearly as sturdy as the henhouse. The
fragile nest wobbled and shook in the wind, which
wriggled through the basketweave and fluffed up
Henrietta's fine feathers.

Suddenly, an even stronger gust blew the
basket right over. It bowled along across the grass,
with Henrietta, her eyes shut tight, clinging on for
dear life.

Splash!

The terrified hen felt a bobbing and a bouncing
beneath her. She sensed a disturbing wetness
around her scrawny toes. She was afloat!

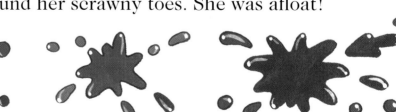

"Help!" squawked Henrietta in the moonlight. "Help! Hen overboard!" Her feet were feeling wetter. She had a horrible feeling that baskets were not at all waterproof.

The next moment, she felt the basket being jostled by several strong beaks. The entire duck family had set sail to help the hapless hen. In less than a minute, they had pushed her to the shore and wedged the basket firmly among some reeds. Henrietta and her precious eggs were safe.

And that is why, if you eavesdrop on a certain busy hen these days, you are likely to hear her talking about "my quackety friends" and "fine farmyard folk, those ducks."

It's just as well that Henrietta can't hear what Durwood the drake says about harebrained hens. But then, a certain busy hen is doing an awful lot of sitting down these days.

The Cluckety Tale of

THE HOPELESS HEN

While Henrietta Hen sat in her basket among the reeds, Little Hen decided she had a chance to make her mark. When Henrietta was around, she made sure that Little Hen well and truly knew her place.

"Little Hen, you are hopeless," she would say. "What kind of an egg do you call that? It's much too pale and long and thin. Can't you lay nice round, brown eggs like mine?"

Well, no, Little Hen couldn't. She could lay beautiful creamy eggs with pointy tops. There was, in fact, nothing wrong with her eggs at all. They just didn't look the same as Henrietta's.

But with Henrietta out of the way, Little Hen's troubles were not over.

"Oh, Little Hen, you are hopeless," said Rudgeworth the rooster. "Your nest is so untidy. You make the whole henhouse look shabby. Can't you make a nice, neat nest like Bettina here?"

Well, no, Little Hen couldn't. She could make big nests that were comfy and warm. There was, in fact, nothing wrong with her nests at all. They just didn't look the same as Bettina's.

Pretty soon, even Bettina, the youngest hen of all, was complaining about Little Hen.

"Oh, Little Hen, you are hopeless," she clucked. "Can't you keep your feathers shiny and bright like mine? You always look as if you've been rooting around in a hedge all morning. You make the whole farmyard look messy."

Well, yes, Little Hen *had* been rooting around in a hedge all morning. She found that was where the very best fat green caterpillars were to be found. And fat green caterpillars were *delicious*. It was true that her feathers didn't look as shiny as Bettina's, but Little Hen was still a pretty little hen with bright eyes and a friendly squawk for everyone.

But the other hens found it very easy to find mean things to say about Little Hen. She was too little. She was too shy. She was too quiet. She was too scruffy. She didn't scratch well. She didn't squawk well. There was no end to it.

Before long, Little Hen believed every cruel word that was said to her. "I really am a hopeless hen," she clucked, as she scuttled across the yard.

After a while, Little Hen didn't bother to come back to the henhouse. She made herself a nest at the bottom of the hedge and sat there in the shade where the other hens couldn't find her. Soon, this made her even sadder.

"No one has come to look for me," she said. "No one cares where I am at all. If I never turned up again, no one would even notice. I might as well just go away."

But Little Hen had never lived anywhere but on Oak Tree Farm. She had no idea where to go, so she stayed in the bottom of the hedge and ate the fat green caterpillars and felt sorry for herself.

Around this time, Farmer Shrive started acting strangely. He looked under upturned buckets. He poked about in the straw in the barn. He even waded through the reeds on the bank of the pond and almost stepped on Henrietta in her basket in the process. He seemed to be looking for something.

"He's lost his watch again," said Durwood Drake. "He's always doing it."

But Farmer Shrive's watch was right there on his wrist as usual.

"He's lost his wallet," said Bettina Hen. "He wouldn't be looking so hard if he hadn't lost lots and lots of money."

"Let's help him find it," said Rudgeworth, who was always eager to keep on Farmer Shrive's good side. He had woken the farmer in the middle of the night once too often, and now often received a serious look from his owner.

Soon every animal and bird on the farm (except Little Hen in her hedge and Henrietta in her basket) was rushing up and down looking for something. Since they had no idea what they were looking for, they looked pretty silly.

Farmer Shrive had no idea why his animals were suddenly acting so oddly. He had only one thing on his mind, and it worried him a great deal.

"I've looked everywhere," he was heard to mutter. "I can't understand it. I do hope we haven't had a visit from that old fox."

Then, one morning, as Farmer Shrive was looking out across his fields, he heard a little rustling sound. Down at the bottom of the hedge, two beady eyes were peering at him.

"Little Hen!" cried Farmer Shrive. "Thank goodness I've found you! My breakfast hasn't been the same without your beautiful, tasty eggs!"

He gathered Little Hen up in his arms and took her right into the farmhouse kitchen, where she sits to this day in her own cardboard box. Not a hopeless hen at all!

The Woofety Tale of

THE DARING DOG

Farmer Shrive had a very clever sheepdog called Diggety. When the sheep went wandering, Diggety rounded them up quickly and efficiently. He was a dog who believed in hard work and no messing around. Farmer Shrive would not have dreamed of having a game of catch with his best worker, or throwing a stick for him to bring back. No, Diggety was a sensible working dog, and that suited everyone concerned.

It was a shock to the farmer and his dog when
they opened the front door one morning and
found a puppy sitting there. While Diggety sniffed
suspiciously at the little one, Farmer Shrive
looked at her collar. There was no address and no
phone number, but there was a name: Alice.

Farmer Shrive was a kind man. He gave the
puppy some food and water and set about finding
out where she belonged. The farmer phoned the
police and the local vet and put up posters around
the area. He thought he would hear from her real
owners very soon.

Three days passed. No one came forward to claim the puppy.

"It's no use, Dig," Farmer Shrive told his old dog, "we'll have to find a new home for her. We can't carry passengers on this farm."

Farmer Shrive called the local animal shelter and told them about Alice.

"I'm sorry," said the woman who answered. "We are full at the moment. Can't you keep her until we have room?"

Reluctantly, Farmer Shrive agreed. "I hope you understand," he said. "We can't keep a dog who doesn't work."

The days passed. The other animals felt sorry for Alice. She was friendlier than Diggety, who could be somewhat stiff and serious.

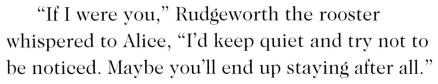

"If I were you," Rudgeworth the rooster whispered to Alice, "I'd keep quiet and try not to be noticed. Maybe you'll end up staying after all."

Alice looked thoughtful ... and did exactly the opposite! From that moment on, she did everything she could to be noticed, especially by the farmer.

One morning, Farmer Shrive looked up from his breakfast to see Alice tightrope-walking along the clothesline!

The next day, he found her trying to dive in the duckpond, which the ducks found very strange.

When Farmer Shrive sat down, tired and aching, after a long day clearing ditches, Alice popped up in front of him and began juggling! Half asleep though he was, Farmer Shrive couldn't help laughing at her antics.

For the next week, there was no end to the daredevil tricks Alice performed. She even

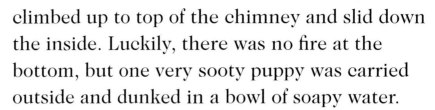

climbed up to top of the chimney and slid down
the inside. Luckily, there was no fire at the
bottom, but one very sooty puppy was carried
outside and dunked in a bowl of soapy water.

"I never know what that little dog will get up to
next," groaned Farmer Shrive. "I'll be glad when
the animal shelter can take her off my hands. Still,
I'd better dry her carefully. I wouldn't want the
little thing to get cold."

The very next day, there was a phone call for
Farmer Shrive. "Yes, I see," the other animals
heard him say. "I'll bring her over in the morning."

But that evening, as Alice snoozed beside him
on the bench outside the back door, the farmer
looked thoughtful. And next morning, as he
backed his old truck out of the barn, he looked
even more worried.

At that moment, he caught sight of Alice carefully herding some ducklings across the yard.

"That little dog brings a lot of fun to this farm," he said to himself. "It makes me smile to see her enjoying herself. And who knows, I might make a sheepdog of her yet. Diggety isn't as young as he was."

So Alice stayed on Oak Tree Farm. She's still there to this day. Although she never has learned to look after sheep, the daring little dog catches every ball that Farmer Shrive throws!

The Baathtime Tale of

THE SHABBY SHEEP

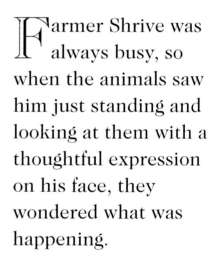

Farmer Shrive was always busy, so when the animals saw him just standing and looking at them with a thoughtful expression on his face, they wondered what was happening.

"He knows what we look like. Why is he *staring*?" muttered Rudgeworth the rooster.

A couple of days later, Rudgeworth felt a little less worried. Farmer Shrive was no

longer looking carefully at the hens and ducks. He
had moved on to the meadow, where he spent a
great deal of time leaning on the fence and looking
long and hard at the sheep.

Sheep are calm creatures most of the time, but
after a while, they too became nervous.

"You don't think he's taking us to maaaaarket,
do you?" Woolhemina asked her cousin Bubble.
"I've never lived anywhere except Oak Tree Farm,
and I don't want to start moving at my age. And
what about all our friends?"

"Aaaaah," said Bubble, trying to look wise. "Maaarket. Aaah."

At that moment, Farmer Shrive seemed to nod his head as if he had come to a decision. He marched toward the farmhouse, calling for his dog Diggety to follow him.

An hour later, Farmer Shrive turned up again and, with the help of Diggety, herded Woolhemina, Bubble, and a small lamb called Jumper into the yard.

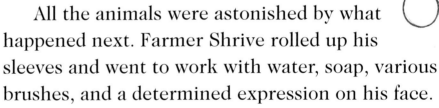

All the animals were astonished by what happened next. Farmer Shrive rolled up his sleeves and went to work with water, soap, various brushes, and a determined expression on his face.

It wasn't easy. Bubble, true to her name, blew bubbles in Farmer Shrive's face, making him splutter and cough. Woolhemina's woolly coat was so tangled that it took all the farmer's strength to brush out the knots and bits of twig and dirt he found there. As for Jumper, you can imagine. One lively lamb, a lot of soapy water, and a slightly slow farmer is a recipe for disaster!

It was almost dark by the time Farmer Shrive had finished. As the moon rose over the yard, Woolhemina, Bubble, and Jumper, their fleeces shining white, were the best-looking, cleanest sheep you have ever seen.

Instead of taking them back to the meadow, Farmer Shrive ushered the animals into an empty stable filled with fresh, clean straw. Then he gave them a good supper, shut the door carefully, and said good night.

Of course, the other animals hurried around. "I must say, you all look lovely," clucked Henrietta Hen, who wasn't always the most tactful creature, "but I'm afraid it must be the market for you. Why else would Farmer Shrive take all this trouble to make you look your best?"

The sheep shuddered and huddled together for comfort. They didn't like what they were hearing one little bit, but they had had a long day and, gradually, as the stars twinkled overhead, they fell asleep in the warm stable.

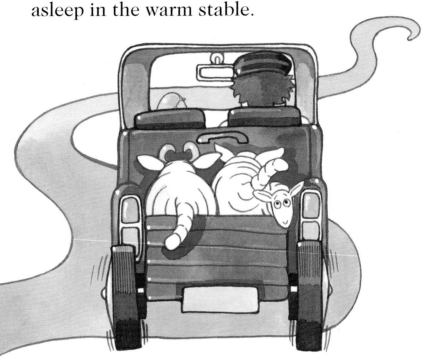

Next morning, Farmer Shrive was up bright and early. He cleaned out the back of his truck and put some clean straw inside. Then he went to the stable with a bucket of soapy water and gave each of the sheep a last tidy-up before leading them into the truck.

"Goodbaaaaa!" bleated Woolhemina, Bubble, and Jumper sadly, as their animal friends gathered to see them off.

As the rumbling of the truck faded in the distance, silence fell over Oak Tree Farm. The usual mooing, clucking, bleating, and quacking stopped.

A couple of hours later, it was still quiet on the farm when a rumbling and rattling was heard again. "He's back," crowed Rudgeworth glumly.

But, to the animals' surprise, Farmer Shrive opened the truck and led out three very familiar and very proud sheep! Each one was wearing a beautiful ribbon, won at the local County Fair, and Farmer Shrive tucked a very handsome silver cup under his arm and headed for the farmhouse with a smile.

The sheep graciously accepted the delighted congratulations of their friends ... before trotting off to the meadow, where there was a particularly muddy patch by the gate. It's all very fine to look lovely, but it isn't always very much fun...

The Moosical Tale of

THE CROTCHETY COWS

Most of the time, the animals on Oak Tree Farm were a cheerful bunch. The ducks and the hens squabbled a bit, and the pigs got a little grumpy if their supper was late, but on the whole they all got along very well. It was a surprise to everyone when the cows became crotchety.

It was a vicious circle. Farmer Shrive happened to mention to Mrs. Moo, the oldest cow of all, that none of the ladies was giving as much milk as usual. Mrs. Moo, who had been happily chewing in the meadow, passed the message on to her friends. Some of the cows were offended and went mooing and muttering to each other, saying what did Farmer Shrive expect with such poor-quality grass to eat?

Other cows got upset. They had been trying as hard as they could, they said, but they could only give as much milk as they could make. As Mrs. Moo said, they weren't milk machines.

Of course, the more troubled the cows became, the less milk they gave. Farmer Shrive got so worried that he called out the vet.

"Which one is it?" hissed Mrs. Moo to her friend Margaret as the vet's van drew up.

"It's Jimmy," mooed Margaret. "Thank goodness for that."

You see, there were two vets who visited Oak Tree Farm. Horace was a big man with red hands who didn't talk much. Although he knew a lot

about animals, he never took the time to talk to his patients, and they didn't like that very much, especially if they were feeling under the weather.

Jimmy, on the other hoof, was young and jolly. He often had something tasty in his pocket, and before he gave any medicine, he always explained exactly what it was. Today, he examined each of the cows gently and thoroughly.

"Well," they heard him say to Farmer Shrive, "there doesn't seem to be much wrong here. It's just one of those things. I've been reading an interesting book about keeping contented animals recently that may give you some ideas. I'll lend you my copy."

Farmer Shrive wasn't much of a reader—he never had the time—but he sat down that evening and didn't go to bed until he had read every page of the vet's book. Although it made him shake his head in some places and laugh out loud in others, he decided that anything was worth a try.

The next morning, Farmer Shrive went over to see his nephew who lived in the village and came back with a big portable stereo system. He put it high up in a tree, out of reach of the inquisitive cows, and turned it on. Something very loud that sounded like a car engine in trouble came out of it. The cows rushed to the other end of the field.

Farmer Shrive twiddled some knobs. A brass band blared out across the grass, causing the cows to shake their heads and try to cover their ears with their hooves.

Finally, after some more twiddling, a swooping, swirling waltz whirled out toward the cows.

Mrs. Moo and her friends looked up. They glanced at each other. Their kind old heads began to sway. And, try as they might, they could not keep their hooves still. One by one, giggling and mooing, the ladies sashayed out across the field, swaying more gracefully than you would ever dream a cow could move.

Farmer Shrive looked on in astonishment.

"I can't believe it will do any good," he said to himself, "but anything is worth a try."

The ladies had a lovely time. Before long, other animals came to join them. The rabbits and ducks had to watch out for the cows' flying feet, of course, but with a whole field to dance in, there was no real problem.

And how they danced! They waltzed, they cha-cha-cha-ed. They tried the Highland fling and the rumba. Melissa tried flamenco but found that it was hard on her hooves. Margaret tried classical

ballet but decided she simply had too many feet. All day the ladies danced, and their friends joined in, applauded, or rested under the trees.

When it was time for evening milking, the ladies were exhausted but very happy … and Farmer Shrive couldn't believe how much milk they gave him!

"Well done, my dears!" he cried. "You're the best milkers in the county!"

Glowing with pride, the ladies went back to their field. And although Farmer Shrive's nephew insisted on taking his stereo back, the cows on Oak Tree Farm continued to be the farmer's pride and joy. (And they even secretly danced the can-can some evenings by the light of the moon!)

The Purrplexing Tale of

THE CURIOUS CAT

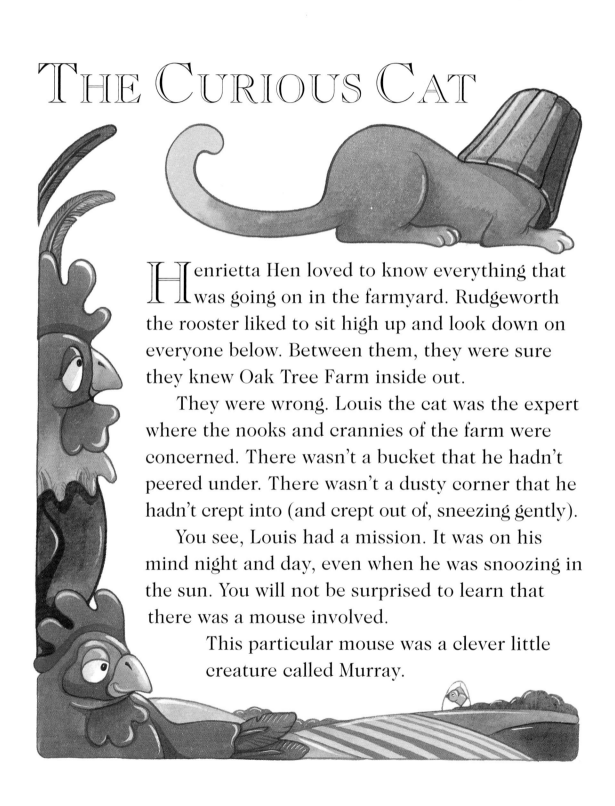

Henrietta Hen loved to know everything that was going on in the farmyard. Rudgeworth the rooster liked to sit high up and look down on everyone below. Between them, they were sure they knew Oak Tree Farm inside out.

They were wrong. Louis the cat was the expert where the nooks and crannies of the farm were concerned. There wasn't a bucket that he hadn't peered under. There wasn't a dusty corner that he hadn't crept into (and crept out of, sneezing gently).

You see, Louis had a mission. It was on his mind night and day, even when he was snoozing in the sun. You will not be surprised to learn that there was a mouse involved.

This particular mouse was a clever little creature called Murray.

Now, Murray had lived on Oak Tree Farm all his life. He had first met Louis the cat when he was just a tiny mouseling. It would be fair to say that it wasn't love at first sight. Louis saw Murray as breakfast. Murray saw Louis as trouble.

Ever since that day, Louis had chased and hunted Murray all over the farm. One day, he was sure, he would catch him. But so far, Murray had always been faster, cleverer, and, let's face it, smaller. Murray could squeeze into spaces that Louis couldn't even get his whiskers into.

Sometimes Murray liked to tease Louis. He would stroll across the yard, just out of reach, and wave his tail casually in the cat's direction.

Louis would leap into action at once, but Murray had his escape route all worked out. Up onto the henhouse, across the roof, a jump onto an overturned bucket, a quick scamper over the straw and through a crack in the wall of the warm stable, right at the back, well away from Alfred the horse's huge hooves.

In vain, Louis would meow and scratch at the wall. He knew he couldn't get in. And Murray would sit smiling and washing his whiskers inside.

The other animals were used to these goings-on. Murray was mischievous and Louis was determined.

There was no prospect of peace in the farmyard with those two around.

But the day came when Murray was nowhere to be seen. Louis slept in the sun, one eye half open as usual, expecting the little mouse to dash out in

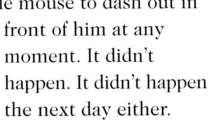

front of him at any moment. It didn't happen. It didn't happen the next day either.

When Murray had not been seen for a whole week, everyone began to worry. So Louis began his search.

It was what Louis called a Serious Search. It involved creeping around all the places that Murray had ever been, listening hard for the scamper of little feet, the squeak of a tiny voice, or even the sneeze of someone washing his whiskers. Louis didn't leave a single nook or cranny unsearched.

Louis was beginning to miss his old sparring
partner badly. Life just wasn't the same without
that naughty little mouse to chase.

All week, Louis searched. He had to tell the
hens, who badly wanted to help, to go back to the
henhouse. It was hard to hear anything with their
scritching and scratching and cackling.

After another couple of days, even Louis was
becoming despondent. His life stretched in front of
him, a boring routine of sleeping and creeping.
Chasing ducklings and chicks just wasn't the
same. They didn't have Murray's spirit of
adventure.

Then, one afternoon, as Louis slept sadly by
the farmhouse door, he thought he heard the
patter of tiny feet right near his nose. At first he
thought he was dreaming, as the pattering went
on. Murray didn't have *that* many feet!

Louis opened one eye and couldn't believe what he was seeing. Across the yard, a whole mouse family was parading proudly. There was a mother mouse at the front, followed by six plump little baby mice and, bringing up the rear and looking as proud as punch, a very familiar little creature. It was Murray!

Then, before Louis's delighted eyes, all eight little mice gave a bold twitch of their tails and scampered off toward the stable. Murray had taught his children well. With a yelp, Louis leaped after them. The fun was just beginning!

The Grunting Tale of

THE GREEDY PIG

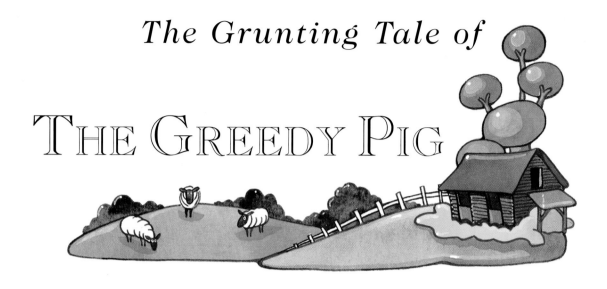

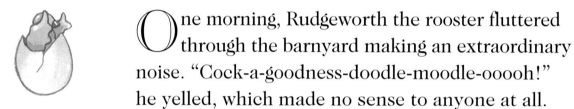

One morning, Rudgeworth the rooster fluttered through the barnyard making an extraordinary noise. "Cock-a-goodness-doodle-moodle-ooooh!" he yelled, which made no sense to anyone at all.

"Take a deep breath, Rudgeworth," said Henrietta, "and tell us calmly what the matter is."

Rudgeworth spluttered and gasped. When he was a little calmer, he said only one sentence, but it was enough to throw everyone else into the same state he had been in. He said, "Pudgy's gate's open."

Henrietta flew off to warn the ducks. The sheep, who had been listening over the wall, rushed back to their meadow. Diggety and Alice put their noses in the air and sniffed, before dashing toward the farmhouse. And several other animals put their heads under their wings or just stood there quivering, not knowing *what* to do.

You see, Pudgy was Farmer Shrive's prize pig, and the fact that the gate to his sty was open meant only one thing: no one's dinner was safe! Pudgy was a prize pig because he *ate*. He ate anything and everything, and when he was roaming around the farmyard, other animals tended to go hungry.

Diggety and Alice had caught Pudgy's scent and ran off to find him. It wasn't difficult. Pudgy's smell was, shall we say, on the strong side.

The dogs found the pig in the kitchen. Farmer Shrive had left his door open when he went out to milk the cows that morning. By the time Alice and Diggety reached him, Pudgy had already eaten a whole loaf of bread, a pie the farmer was saving for supper, three eggs (including the shells), a bucket of potatoes, and half a dozen apples from a bowl on the table.

In the process, Pudgy had, well, totally rearranged the kitchen. It was a horrible mess.

"Pudgy!" barked Diggety angrily, but the pig was already on his way, waddling across the floor. He had just spotted a large bag of dog biscuits near the open door. They looked pretty tasty.

This was too much for Diggety. He had been fairly angry at the mess Pudgy had made in the kitchen, but when a dog can't call his own biscuits his own…

Out in the farmyard, the other animals heard a terrible din. There was barking and squealing and more barking (from Alice this time) and a lot more squealing. Then, tearing out of the farmhouse came Pudgy, moving at a speed no pig is built for, with Diggety firmly attached by his teeth to the end of the pig's curly little tail.

Pudgy tore around the farmyard so fast that steam began to rise from his trotters. Diggety held on grimly.

"What are we going to do?" squawked Rudgeworth, appalled.

As usual, Henrietta Hen had an idea.

"Well, well!" she called out, in her loudest screech. "I never thought I'd see the day when a pig could outrun a sheepdog!"

Diggety rose to the challenge. "He's not outrunning me!" he woofed, realizing too late that in order to reply he had removed his teeth from Pudgy's tail. The pig scurried back into his sty and leaned against the gate to keep it shut.

Diggety slowed to a stop and hung his head.

"You should be ashamed, Diggety Dog," said Henrietta. "What were you thinking? You know the rule: no biting!"

"But he was eating my biscuits!" whined Diggety. "And you should see the mess he's made in Farmer Shrive's kitchen!"

One by one, the animals trooped across the yard and looked in at the open door. It was a terrible sight.

"Pudgy doesn't mean to make a mess," said Alice slowly. "He is a pig, after all."

"And it's our job as animals to make sure this farm runs smoothly," said Henrietta, looking severely at Diggety. "Now, you all know what you have to do."

Working together, the animals put the kitchen back in order. They couldn't do anything about the bread, the potatoes, the pie, the apples, or the eggs, but everything else soon looked perfect.

And Pudgy Pig, whose tail already felt better, went to sleep dreaming of dog biscuits. Diggety trotted off and told his friends the sheep all about it, until he felt better, too.

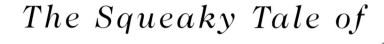

The Squeaky Tale of

THE TOO-MANY MICE

Louis the cat, you will remember, was delighted when Murray Mouse started a family. It just meant more fun for Louis. But mouse families are large … and they tend to get larger. Only a few weeks later, it seemed, Murray Mouse became the proud grandfather of thirty-five little mouselings!

At first, Louis couldn't believe his luck. Everywhere he went, a little twitchety nose would poke out from behind a sack of grain or a flowerpot. Whenever he opened one eye after a snooze in the sun, two or three little twitchety tails would whisk away out of sight. It was enough to gladden the heart of any cat, but for a cat like Louis who lived to chase mice, it was sheer heaven.

But not very long after Murray became a grandfather, his grandchildren had children, too. Now Murray was a great-grandfather, and Louis was an increasingly worried cat. By the end of each day of dashing and pouncing, he was absolutely exhausted.

"What's the matter?" woofed Diggety, seeing Louis dragging himself across the yard without the usual catlike spring in his step. "Not feeling too well? You're starting to feel your age, like me!"

Louis arched his back disdainfully. "I certainly am not!" he declared. "But have you noticed how this place is overrun with mice? It's a disgrace!"

"You're the disgrace!" laughed Alice, who could sometimes be a little thoughtless. "I understood cats were supposed to make sure there weren't too many mice! You're not doing your job, lazy Louis!"

Now this really was unfair. In fact, just then Louis was the least lazy animal on the whole farm. He was pouncing his paws off.

Poor Louis's problems were just beginning. By the end of the year, Murray Mouse was a great-great-great-great-great-grandfather, as well as having almost a hundred more children himself. Even the other animals on the farm began to complain about the numbers of mice in the yard, in the barn, in the stables, in the sty, in the henhouse, and even in the farmhouse itself.

As for Louis, he was a shadow of his former self, and he was worried, too. He knew that it was only a matter of time before Farmer Shrive noticed the number of mice around the place and started to blame Louis for it.

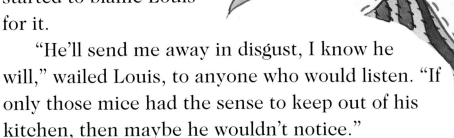

"He'll send me away in disgust, I know he will," wailed Louis, to anyone who would listen. "If only those mice had the sense to keep out of his kitchen, then maybe he wouldn't notice."

As a matter of fact, Farmer Shrive had already noticed. It wasn't the nibbles in pies that bothered him. He was usually much too busy to notice things like that. No, it was the skittering and scattering that kept him awake at night as several hundred hungry mice pattered across the attic floor. That really drove him wild.

One morning, Louis's worst fears were realized. Farmer Shrive stomped downstairs in a horribly bad mood and growled as he almost fell over an exhausted cat in the doorway.

"If you did *less* sleeping, I might do more, Louis!" he grunted. "Things have gone too far! It's time I got another cat!"

"Goodbye, old friend," Louis told Diggety that morning. "I'll be on my way pretty soon. If only Murray's children didn't all want to stay *here* to raise their families. Why don't they go somewhere else and find homes of their own?"

"I think they find it just a little too … er … comfortable here," said Diggety. "I mean, it's a nice safe place to raise mouselings, isn't it?" Seeing Louis's face, he didn't go on, but his meaning was clear. With only a tired cat on the

premises, those mice had never been safer. There was absolutely no reason why they would want to move. And they didn't.

For the rest of the day, Louis didn't even bother to try chasing the mice. He wandered around saying goodbye to all the other animals in the farmyard. "Farmer Shrive has gone out to buy a leaner, fitter, younger cat," he said sadly. "You'll probably like him better than a tired old cat like me. In a few weeks you probably won't even remember I was here."

That afternoon, as Louis had predicted, the leaner, fitter, younger cat arrived. But he wasn't anything like what Louis had expected. In fact, he wasn't a he at all. He was a she!

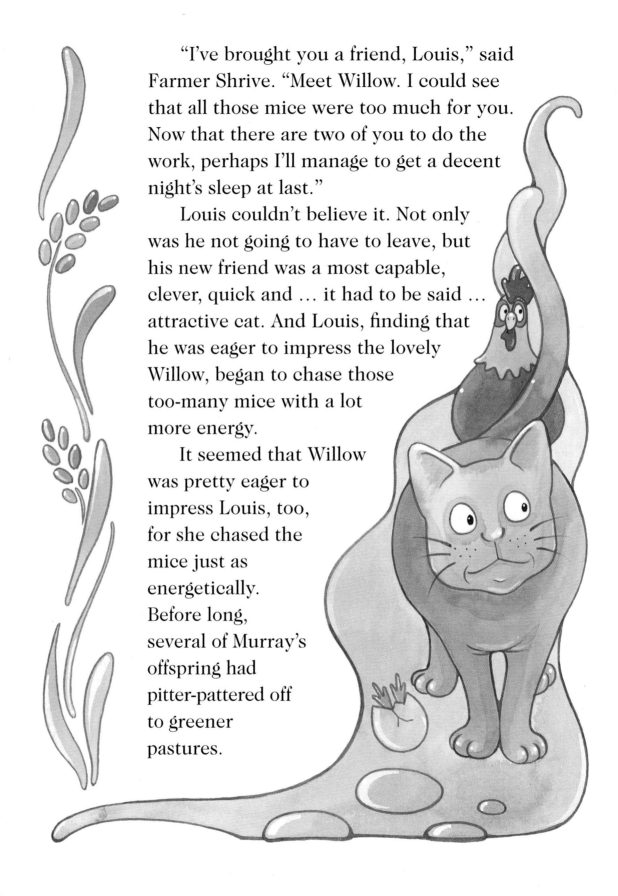

"I've brought you a friend, Louis," said Farmer Shrive. "Meet Willow. I could see that all those mice were too much for you. Now that there are two of you to do the work, perhaps I'll manage to get a decent night's sleep at last."

Louis couldn't believe it. Not only was he not going to have to leave, but his new friend was a most capable, clever, quick and … it had to be said … attractive cat. And Louis, finding that he was eager to impress the lovely Willow, began to chase those too-many mice with a lot more energy.

It seemed that Willow was pretty eager to impress Louis, too, for she chased the mice just as energetically. Before long, several of Murray's offspring had pitter-pattered off to greener pastures.

One day Rudgeworth the rooster found Louis pacing up and down outside the barn. "Now don't start taking it easy," he warned, "just because one or two of those mice have gone away. There are still lots of them left. You and Willow will still have to work hard to keep them in check."

But Louis, who had heard some little sounds inside the barn, had begun to smile.

"I don't think it will be a problem," he grinned. "We're bringing in reinforcements. Come and meet them!"

He led the surprised rooster into the barn, where five furry little bundles were curled up next to their mother.

"Mouse-chasers every one," purred their proud father.

The Snuffly Tale of
THE BARNYARD BUNNIES

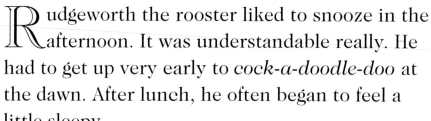

Rudgeworth the rooster liked to snooze in the afternoon. It was understandable really. He had to get up very early to *cock-a-doodle-doo* at the dawn. After lunch, he often began to feel a little sleepy.

Rudgeworth had long ago discovered that the henhouse was not the place for an afternoon nap. Henrietta and her friends were often there, chatting and scratching. Little chicks or naughty mice would peek in and scuffle through the straw. It was distracting to a senior bird, and Rudgeworth set out to find a better place to sleep.

In the end, the stable turned out to be the best spot. There was lots of snuggly straw and quietness. Better still, old Alfred the horse often had a snooze himself, so there was no danger of a resting rooster being stomped on by a heavy hoof. For several years, Alfred and Rudgeworth dreamed the afternoons away in peace.

Then, one rainy afternoon, when the stable was particularly warm and comfortable, Rudgeworth was woken from his nap by a small sound in the corner. It wasn't the scuttling of the occasional mouse—he had become used to that. It wasn't the swish of Alfred's tail or the tiniest snore from an elderly horse. It was a kind of snuffling, sniffing sound. The more Rudgeworth listened, the surer he became that someone in the corner was quietly crying.

Now, Rudgeworth could be brash and was not always too sensitive (especially to Farmer Shrive's sleeping habits), but he didn't like to see—or even hear—another animal in distress.

"Who's there?" he whispered, not wanting to wake Alfred. "Can I help?"

More sniffing from the corner.

"Don't cry!" hissed Rudgeworth. "I'm coming over. Stay where you are."

Rustling as quietly as he could through the deep straw, Rudgeworth reached the corner of the barn. He pushed the straw aside with his wings and beak.

There, huddled in the corner, were not one but two little bunnies. Rudgeworth was startled. There were lots of rabbits on the farm, but this was the first time the rooster had seen any coming into the barnyard. Surely, after the mouse problem, there wasn't going to be a bunny problem?

"Don't cry," said Rudgeworth again. "Tell me what the matter is. I might be able to help. Are you lost?"

The bunnies shook their heads. "We're not crying," one of them whispered. "We've just got snuffles in our noses."

"Snuffles in your noses?" repeated Rudgeworth. He had a beak, not a nose, so he wasn't sure what this meant. He had a vague idea that snuffles were some kind of tiny insects that crawled into places they weren't wanted.

"Yes, we caught cold in all this rain," said the other bunny, "and now we can't stop sniffling and snuffling and … and … *ah-chooooo* … sneezing!"

"I see," said Rudgeworth, when he had rearranged his feathers. "Well, of course, you can't go out in the rain when you're not feeling well. You can just stay quietly in this corner until you are better."

But quietness was something those poor bunnies couldn't manage. Once one of them started sneezing, the other couldn't hold back. Soon they were both sneezing several times a minute.

"What *is* all this noise?" asked a deep voice. "Can't a horse snooze in his own stable these days?"

Rudgeworth quickly explained the situation to Alfred. "Well, I feel sorry for you, of course," he said, "but you can't stay here."

Rudgeworth, worried that Alfred might ban *any* visitors if he was annoyed any further, spread out his wings and spoke kindly to the bunnies. "Come on," he said, "one under each wing. We'll find you somewhere else to sit until the weather improves."

Rudgeworth and the bunnies made a strange sight as they crossed the barnyard ... and crossed it again ... and again ... and again. No one wanted sneezing bunnies in their henhouse, barn, or sty.

"I don't want my kittens to catch cold," said Louis the cat. "And I'm sure any father would feel the same way."

"I wouldn't know about that," replied the rooster. "Henrietta is still sitting on our eggs. It seems to be taking ages."

Rudgeworth hunted the whole barnyard, but he couldn't find a single place for the bunnies, who were still sneezing and sniffling at every step, to stay. Finally, there was only one place left. "Come with me," said Rudgeworth.

And that is why, when Farmer Shrive went into his spare bedroom that evening to look for his second-best boots, he was surprised to find two little bunnies tucked up snugly under the quilt. He didn't have the heart to disturb them.

Maybe it was Farmer Shrive's good conscience that meant he slept especially well that night. Or maybe it was the fact that Rudgeworth the rooster didn't crow at dawn as usual. A certain bird found that those annoying little snuffles insects had found their way into *his* beak, as well!

The Whinnysome Tale of

THE PERFECT PONY

When Farmer Shrive cleared out the stable next to Alfred's one morning, everyone was curious. The clearing out took a long time. Over the years, the farmer had put lots of things he thought he just *might* need in the future out of sight in the old stable.

Out came a bicycle with only one wheel, five cans of pink paint, a ladder with several rungs missing, an old lantern, a wheelbarrow with a hole in it, two and a half pairs of rubber boots, an old jacket, and several cardboard boxes full of useful things. At least, that's what Farmer Shrive thought they were.

For a while, the animals were much too interested in all this stuff to ask the really important question. It was, of course, that nosy (or beaky) hen Henrietta, who happened to wander into the barnyard for something to eat, who asked, "Why is Farmer Shrive emptying that stable? Is something—or someone—else going into it?"

As soon as she said it, there was flapping and quacking and clucking and snorting and snuffling all around. Was someone new coming to the farm? Would it be another huge horse, like Alfred?

Henrietta shivered. "Those giant feet," she moaned, "and my tiny chicks. I can't bear to think about it."

Unfortunately, Alfred overheard her. (Henrietta's voice always was a bit piercing.)

"I'll have you know that I have never, ever stood on a little one," he said. "I am extremely dainty in my footwork. I resent your tone, Mrs. Hen. I resent it very much indeed."

While Alfred retired to the back of his stable in a huff, the other animals peered into the empty stable next door. Farmer Shrive swept it carefully. Then he brought in a load of sweet, new straw and spread it over the floor.

The animals looked at each other. There was no doubt about it now. *Someone* was moving in!

They didn't have long to wait. Before lunch, a trailer pulled up in the barnyard and Farmer Shrive threw open the doors. Out trotted a pretty little cream pony, with a dark mane and tail. She tossed her head, took a good look around the farmyard, and trotted neatly into her stable.

"Perfect!" beamed Farmer Shrive, looking over the door. "Absolutely perfect!"

While the farmer went into the farmhouse for his lunch, the other animals gathered outside the stable. The smaller ones sat on the shoulders of the larger ones so that they could see in. Alfred began to wish that he had not been sulking in the back of his stable when the stranger arrived. He was the only animal who had not seen her.

Rudgeworth kindly supplied a running commentary for his old friend. "She's charming. Really charming. And Farmer Shrive thinks she's perfect. I heard him say so. Twice!"

Alfred snorted. For many years now he had been the only horse on Oak Tree Farm. The other animals looked up to him. But here was a frisky newcomer. And why on earth did Farmer Shrive want her? She couldn't pull the cart that Alfred sometimes pulled in parades and shows, could she? Surely Farmer Shrive wasn't going to ride her! Rudgeworth said she was a fairly small pony, and he was a fairly large farmer.

All the same, Alfred was worried. He swung his big head over his door and tried to peer around into the next stable.

"Oh! Ow!" At exactly the same moment, the new pony had looked out and tried to peer into Alfred's stable. Alfred's nose bumped the pony's head. The animals who had been stretching to look at the newcomer jumped back in alarm and all fell over into the yard.

When the confusion had died down, Alfred and the pony, whose name was Lucy, introduced themselves. Alfred couldn't think of a polite way of asking why Lucy had come to Oak Tree Farm, so he asked anyway.

"Why are you here?" he asked bluntly.

"Because I'm perfect," trilled the pony. "That's what the farmer said. He took one look at me at the show and said, 'She's perfect! I'll take her!'"

Alfred snorted. Durwood the drake giggled. To his mind, an animal without webbed feet could hardly be called perfect.

"Sometimes," said Little Hen, trying to be helpful, "people just buy things because they are beautiful. Like pictures … and flowers … and hats!"

Alfred gave her a despairing look. "Farmer Shrive has never bought a beautiful hat in his life. Don't talk nonsense, Little Hen. Everyone on this farm works hard. What's Lucy going to do?"

No one knew, but the next day things went from bad to worse. Farmer Shrive led Lucy out into the barnyard and brushed her coat. He polished her hooves and combed her mane. Then, to everyone's astonishment, he began to braid it and put little pink ribbons in it!

"You see," squawked Little Hen triumphantly, "just like you might put on a beautiful hat. What did I tell you?"

Alfred scowled. Farmer Shrive looked after him well, but seeing all this attention being given to a little pony, the old horse felt distinctly jealous. Was the farmer going to spend hours grooming young Lucy *every* day?

At that moment, another car drew into the barnyard. Out hopped Farmer Shrive's niece and her parents.

"Happy Birthday, Charlotte!" cried Farmer Shrive. "Your parents asked me if I could keep this big surprise for you until your special day. What do you think?"

Charlotte ran and threw her arms around Lucy. They could hardly hear her excited voice with her face buried in Lucy's mane.

"Oh, thank you!" she said. "She's perfect!"

Later that day, after Lucy and her new family had left, Farmer Shrive put all his old junk … sorry, *useful things* … back into the stable.

"Back to normal, old friend," he told Alfred with a smile. "I like it that way." The horse rested his big head on Farmer Shrive's shoulder for a moment. He liked it, too.

The Honking Tale of

THE GRATEFUL GEESE

Not all the animals on Oak Tree Farm belonged to Farmer Shrive. Strictly speaking, the too-many-mice just happened to live there—to the annoyance of everyone except Louis the cat and his family. The little birds that boldly flew in and pecked at the hens' food were the same. But it was rare for the farm to have other wild visitors.

One day, two big white birds flew high overhead, circled, and came down to rest among the reeds beside the duckpond.

There was immediate concern from the ducks. These birds were *huge*. Durwood the drake hurried the little ones to the opposite bank and settled down behind some reeds of his own to peer at the newcomers.

"They're *geese*," hissed Henrietta Hen, who had scuttled up beside him.

"I *know*," muttered Durwood. "But why are they *here*? I've often seen them passing over, but they never stop."

All day, the farmyard animals watched the geese. They didn't do anything much. They sat by the bank, pecked at some greenery from time to time, and occasionally stretched their wings.

Durwood was full of foreboding. "I don't like it," he said. "I don't like it at all." As dusk began to fall on the farmyard, he stayed at his post, watching the visitors' every move. Henrietta, who always had to poke her beak into any interesting event, popped by frequently.

Then, to his great astonishment, he saw a single bird strutting toward the geese. It was Rudgeworth the rooster!

"What's he *doing*?" screeched Henrietta Hen. "Is he mad? Who knows what they'll do to him. Oh dear, oh dear! I've squawked some harsh things about Rudgeworth in my time, but really he's the dearest, sweetest bird. Oh, Rudgeworth! And he still has such a bad cold, too!"

Henrietta's husband appeared unconcerned (if a little snuffly around the beak). It looked as if he was chatting pleasantly with the geese on the other side of the pond. After a few minutes, the rooster flapped his wings, gave a subdued crow of agreement, and strutted back to Alfred's stable, where he was sniffing and snuffling quietly, away from the hurly-burly of the henhouse.

While Henrietta hurried off to interrogate Rudgeworth, the geese rested a little more, until Farmer Shrive was spotted chugging back from the far field on his tractor. No sooner had he turned the engine off in the yard than the most alarming noise began at the edge of the pond. Those geese honked. They hissed. They squawked and shouted. They ran up and down and flapped their wings. The sound was ghastly. Many of the smaller animals were so upset that they started squealing and snorting themselves.

Farmer Shrive nearly jumped out of his boots. He tried waving his arms at the geese and shouting, but it had no effect except to make the visitors even more excited. Finally, red in the face, the farmer went into the farmhouse and slammed the door. But the noise went on.

Late into the night, the squawking, honking, hissing and screeching continued. Around midnight, there was a brief pause. Just long enough for Farmer Shrive to get to sleep ... and then the terrible din started again. The poor farmer even came outside to throw water over the noisy birds—with no effect.

Meanwhile, snug in Alfred's stable, Rudgeworth the rooster seemed strangely happy—for a bird who was snuffling and sniffling and sneezing the night away.

The next morning, peace reigned at last. Rudgeworth didn't feel like having breakfast, but his friends by the pond were more than happy to eat it for him.

"Thanks for letting us stay," said one of them. "Our trip north for the summer is exhausting. I just couldn't have flown another flap."

"You're welcome," replied Rudgeworth. "I was worried that Farmer Shrive would get used to the quiet while I was ill and might want to get rid of me when I started crowing again. Now he'll be relieved to hear me! See you next year!"

The Zzzzzzzzz Tale of
The Too-Tired Farmer

Farmer Shrive was so relieved when the noise of the honking geese stopped, he gave a little dance for joy. Then, exhausted after a night of listening to the pandemonium by the pond, he fell into bed and was soon asleep, although it was already morning.

He must have been a very tired farmer. He slept through morning milking, feeding the hens, collecting the eggs, feeding the pigs, checking the sheep, feeding Alfred, checking the ducks, feeding

Diggety and Alice, and opening the gates for the milk-tanker. He slept all the way through the morning, and the afternoon, and the evening, too. Then, as the moon rose in the sky, he slept all the way through the night as well. It was the most sleep he had had for many a year.

Under the shining stars, the animals of Oak Tree Farm slept too, but they had had a very busy day. Quietly and carefully (but with a little quiet squawking from Henrietta Hen, whose chicks seemed to get *everywhere*), they did all the work on the farm. Milking the cows (twice) was the hardest part, but Mrs. Moo and the other ladies were as helpful as could be. After all, they knew the routine.

When the sky in the east began to glow with an orange light that promised a whole new day, someone woke up. He found, to his delight, that there were no snuffles or sniffles in his beak at all. Grinning, he flapped up to the top of the henhouse and threw back his head.

Cock-a-doodle-doo!

Farmer Shrive sat up in bed and smiled. He felt rested. He felt well. He felt glad to be alive. And he felt surprisingly friendly to a certain raucous rooster on a nearby roof.

As the day dawned, the fact that he had slept a whole day and a whole night dawned on Farmer Shrive. Worried about his animals, he rushed downstairs and out into the yard. All was well. Everyone looked contented, and Mrs. Moo and the ladies were lined up behind the gate as usual.

Farmer Shrive smiled again (and two smiles before breakfast were unheard of from him). A farm that runs itself ... every farmer's dream.

Out in the yard, the animals were glad to see the farmer so happy.

"It's funny the way humans never realize that we keep everything going for them," said Henrietta, watching a naughty chick tickling Diggety Dog's nose.

"What they don't know can't hurt them," agreed Rudgeworth, nodding his head wisely. "And what they don't know is an awful lot!"

Maybe it would be better if you *didn't* lend this book to Farmer Shrive... OK?